Stephen King Stephen King

Stephen King Stephen King

William Walsh

Portions of *Stephen King Stephen King* previously appeared in *Necessary Fiction, The Kenyon Review Blog, Quick Fiction, The Morning News, BOAAT*, and *The Boston Literary Review.*

Cover design by Peter Cole.

ISBN 978-0-692-83815-0

Table of Contents

Kidz Love Klezmer 7

Sleepwalking Man 9

Stephen King Stephen King 13

Simpsons Marathon 17

A Set of Objects, a Situation, a Chain of Events which shall be the Formula of a Particular Emotion; Such that when the External Facts, which must Terminate in Sensory Experience, are Given, the Emotion is Immediately Evoked 21

Portions Toll 23

Pegs 25

Narration, Character, Consequence 29

Workshop 31

Contemporary Short Story 33

Requited 37

Calendar Sisters   41

Direct Address   43

Rosencrantz and Guildenstern Are Wed   47

Boy Toat   53

Chaos   55

Sibella   57

DOB/RIP   61

Gallop   65

Twin Thing   67

My Secret Brand   71

Chick Magnet   73

Seven Personifications   77

Emily Dickinson As If   79

Mothers, a Drabble   81

Comfort Food   83

Tonsure   87

Scale   89

Analog   93

Head Heart Hands Feet   95

The Kennedys   99

Kidz Love Klezmer

Look at little Gene dance. Spinning. Swinging his arms. Kicking out. His head down and then up. Look at his face. He's ecstatic. What's going through his mind? I call out to little Gene, This is a kolomeike, my boy. All the other kids are watching Gene dance. They are dancing like Gene. Kids love klezmer—it's true! Gene is pretending to play the accordion as he dances. His elbows are pumping. My wife wouldn't come today. She said, Kids don't like klezmer. I told her she couldn't be more wrong. I told her, The event is named Kidz Love Klezmer. She waved her hands in my face dismissively. She said, You can take him—I'm not stopping you! Now they're forming the kids in a circle for a freylekh. Little Gene is the lucky duck between two cuties, sisters Delia and Rose Humphrey. He's trying hard to catch his breath. His face is red. All of the kids are red-faced and breathing heavily. But smiling. And dancing. I sneak a peek at the man playing upright bass. His hat is pulled low on his forehead. He wears oversized glasses. He plays his instrument like a dance partner. He never takes his eyes off the little man on the snare drum. And I'm clapping along and I didn't even realize. A sher and a khusidl and a zhok and a sirba. I'm not the only parent transfixed by this whirling, dancing sight. We're all speechless. I feel as though the dancing of the

children could levitate the hall. The children are glowing. The musicians must be exhausted. The clarinet and the accordion are brothers, I see. Big, fat men with curly, klezmer hair. Little Gene is guzzling from the water bottle that's passing around. His legs keep moving as he pours the water over his head. I am clapping in time to the snare drum and stomping my foot to the upright bass. And I see across the hall that my wife has come! In spite of all that she had said. She's here. I race over to the entrance and pick her up off her feet. I kiss her face and give her a chiropractic hug. I want to hug the juice out of her and drink it down! Look at little Gene, I say. He loves klezmer! All of the parents begin to dance with their kids. We form a circle of a hundred. Maybe more. We dance clockwise and then on cue we dance counterclockwise. Then we break off into dozens of tight family circles and dance faster circles. The band is playing louder and faster. The music crashes to a halt and the children cheer and fall to the ground. I bend to look into little Gene's face. I've never seen such exhaustion, such joy. His eyes are focused on the twinkling lights that hang from high ceiling. I ask him, What do you see, Gene? He says, Fireworks. Like it's the Fourth of July.

Sleepwalking Man

Dan Morone gets up at the sound of the alarm clock and makes his way to the kitchen. He starts the coffeemaker. He knows that he's still sleeping. He laughs. His wife kisses him on the cheek on her way to the coffeemaker.

Wake up, Dan, she says.

Dan laughs. I'm awake, he says.

But Dan is still sleeping as he showers, shaves, and gets dressed for the office. He looks in the full length mirror and tells himself to wake up. Then he laughs.

The bus stop is unoccupied until the woman with the pillow for a face arrives. She smiles at Dan and says, Good morning.

Dan says, I'm still sleeping. Then he laughs.

On the bus, Dan sleeps through his stop. He has to walk a few blocks back to his office. He bumps into a few people along the way and almost steps into traffic. He laughs at the sound of the car horns in the street.

Dan puts his head down on his desk. Something is wrong with his computer. The thermos he brought from home is empty.

He forgot to put on socks. There's a bird flying though the office but nobody notices. Dan laughs.

Elaine, his officemate, says, You're doing it again, Dan.

Dan says, I'm awake. He laughs and Elaine laughs. She makes a loud snoring sound and then Dan makes a loud snoring sound.

Dan's boss calls him upstairs. Bring the quarterly report, he says.

Funny thing about the quarterly report: It was done and printed days ago—at the close of the quarter. But Dan can't find it.

Elaine says, Wake up, Dan. You're sitting on the quarterly report.

Dan's boss comes to work without clothes on. Nobody in the office says anything about it. His hair is red, his face is red, and the walls of his large office are red.

You look tired, Dan's boss says.

Dan laughs. I'm awake, he says.

Dan's boss flips through the pages of the quarterly report and floats to the ceiling. He says to Dan, I am happy with these numbers.

Dan's standing in front of the snack machine in the break-room, thinking of the way his backyard used to smell when his mom was doing laundry in the basement. One day he traced the source of the scent to the dryer vent. He curled himself around the dryer vent and fell asleep beneath its warm exhaust.

Fuller, the IT guy, puts a dollar into the snack machine and makes his selection. Dan watches Fuller's M&Ms fall from the snack rack. Fuller says, Wake up, Dan.

Dan calls home and his wife picks up quickly, before the first ring is complete. She whispers, Hello.

Dan says, Hi, honey.

Dan, she says, still whispering. The baby is napping. Don't call during naptime.

She hangs up the phone quietly.

Dan laughs.

Elaine says, What's so funny, Dan?

Dan says, It's baby's naptime.

Stephen King Stephen King

My wife and I have been engaged in a game of Stephen King since the earliest days of our marriage.

The game began when we moved into our first home. The real estate agent described the house as pre-Colonial, and it *was* primitive. We wrote an offer for the house on a sunny day. We moved in during a three-day thunder storm. The previous owners left behind a sort of housewarming gift: Two shopping bags filled with Stephen King paperbacks. There was at least one copy of each of his books, and multiple copies of his really popular titles, like *Carrie, Cujo,* and *The Shining*. The bags even contained his pseudonymous books, written under the names Richard Bachman, John Swithen, and Cleo Birdwell.

My wife didn't want to throw the books away, so she put them in the basement. I thought it would be funny to place the books on the dining room table one evening and deny that I had put them there. Then I thought it would be funny if I put the Stephen Kings in the refrigerator and deny that I had put them there. She retaliated one night by filling my pillowcase with the Stephen Kings. She still denies having put them there.

Stephen King soon evolved into a game of hide and scream. One of us would hide on the other and then jump from the hiding place and scream, Stephen King. And Stephen

King was also a game of whispers. If my wife dozed off in the living room on a given night, I would whisper in her ear, over and over, until she would wake, Stephen King, Stephen King, Stephen King.

In the early years, we never got tired of playing Stephen King. We played Stephen King at home and we played Stephen King in restaurants, shopping malls, airports, and hotels. We played Stephen King so much that we could have turned pro.

At some point, my wife added a physical element to Stephen King. She would strike me with one of his books or sometimes her hand. Two examples:

1) At the new Target that opened in town, my wife likes to wait until our paths diverge, then she will circle back to the book section to find the latest from Stephen King. She will sneak up behind me, hit me on the back of the head with the book and shout, Stephen King.

2) Stephen King goes to every Red Sox home-game, and he can often be seen in the stands when the camera is positioned to shoot a left-handed batter. If my wife sees Stephen King in the frame, she'll pause the TV and punch me on the arm as she shouts, Stephen King.

I took my game of Stephen King in a more cerebral direction. Two examples:

1) A guy I work with has a practice of painting a new portrait of Stephen King every time King updates his press photo. He's done dozens of Stephen King portraits, painted in oils, acrylics, dry-brush watercolors, gouache, and airbrush. One night when my wife was out, I hung these Stephen King portraits, gallery-like, in place of all our family photos.

2) When our first child was born and just home from the hospital, I swaddled a copy of *Firestarter* in her pink receiving blanket and approached my wife in a panicked state. I said, There is something wrong with the baby. My alarmed wife

said, What's wrong? I said, She's on fire! And I tossed the blanketed book to her, shouting, Stephen King!

We've had several Stephen King truces and a yearlong Stephen King détente right after the author was struck by a motor vehicle and nearly killed while out for an evening walk near his home in Lovell, Maine. In the last year or two, Stephen King has become a game via email, a midnight Facebook update, a ritual observed on Halloween, or just a shared laugh when we see the woman in town who looks just like Stephen King, with her spooky rectangular head, her short men's haircut, and her squarish Stephen King eyeglasses from the Stephen King Collection at LensCrafters.

Our kids play Stephen King now more than we do. Just last weekend I overheard our daughters jumping rope in the garage. They sang a little rhyme over and over as they jumped. The rhyme went like this:

Stephen King, Stephen King.
You're afraid of everything.
Stephen King, Stephen King.
You're afraid of everything.

Simpsons Marathon

Marge almost runs over Homer pulling her car into the garage. Bart says, What's shakin' Santa? Grandpa's dentures are stolen by a turtle, and Grandpa can't catch the turtle. Lisa has a dream about riding on a talking giraffe. Maggie possesses an abstract, expressionless face. Reverend Lovejoy is voiced by Harry Shearer. Marge promises Homer a tonguebath. Ned Flanders believes that the best part of Jesus' facial hair was the mustache. Springfield gets a monorail. Bart writes on the chalkboard: I will not whistle while walking past the graveyard. Homer is mistaken for Bigfoot. Ralphie Wiggams says, My cat's breath smells like catfood. Bart finds a blackhead gun at Patty and Selma's house, holds it like a gangster, and says, Stick 'em up. Krusty the Clown smokes a menthol. Lisa goes to the library and checks out *Snow White*, by Donald Barthelme. At birth, Bart scores 1 out of 10 on the APGAR scale. Homer goes to the Kwik-E-Mart for a Squishy and a SlimJim. Matt Groenig says, The course of serial narrative is as follows: primitive, classic, baroque, and decadent. The *Treehouse of Horrors* episode airs the week after Halloween. We learn that Marge's maiden name is Bouvier. Sideshow Bob tries to murder Bart. Ms. Krabappel goes to Staples and buys a stapler. Bart orders a spy camera and it comes in the mail. Doctor Julius Hibbert tells Homer he has

spoon-in-mouth disease, and then he chuckles. This episode of Itchy and Scratchy is entitled *Sodom and Tomorrow*. The fish Bart catches has three eyes from nuclear waste. Homer's T-shirt says, No Fat Chicks. Otto Mann's T-shirt says, I smoked an acre of Jamaica. Lisa explains that mules are sterile but not impotent. Homer takes Marge to Ye Olde Off-Ramp Inn. Barney Gumble burps. Bart is almost kept back in fourth grade. Homer tells Bart, You think it was her tits that made you look twice but it was really her shoulders. Mr. Burns says, Smithers, release the hounds. Mr. Burns says, Excellent. Mr. Burns says, Boffo. Mr. Burns says, Is he one of ours? Patty and Selma favor an Eastern European douche that contains extract of cabbage. Homer says, Doe, and then Lisa points at a deer and says, A deer, and then Marge clarifies, A female deer. Ned Flanders likes to call his mustache Mr. Womb-Broom. Bart shakes his head and says, Charlie Brown's leitmotiv—good grief. Homer uses a hair growth tonic to grow a full head of hair and gets a promotion. Twelve o'clock and all is hell, shouts Groundskeeper Willie to an empty elementary school. Marge's painting depicts a forest of shoe trees. Maggie squeaks her binky. Homer says, Exiting was my exit strategy. Dancin' Homer becomes the team mascot for the Springfield Isotopes. Patty agrees with Selma: Panties or perfume—never both. Homer puts on a pair of eyeglasses but does not look smarter. Bart watches a documentary about a Canadian humorist who teaches his five-year-old son to say funny instead of laughing. Mentally, the medium Duff T-shirt still fits Homer. Ralphie's shirt is inside out and backwards. Lisa asks the applepicker how he deals with the symbolism all day long. Marge invents a boardgame called *Approximate Anagrams* that let's everybody be a winner. Lisa has a new mantra: I am quiet as a pearl. Marge makes her own mayonnaise, so—long story short—Homer's race to three hundred pounds began the day they got married. Principal Skinner has a Vietnam flashback. Principal Skinner has

an acid flashback. Principal Skinner has a Bart flashback. In a practiced stage-whisper, Marge says, Nobody credits me for my irony. Ned Flanders believes that an obnoxious mustache is a successful mustache. Milhouse is the kid in school with the smallest pencil—like, ridiculously small. Homer doesn't like to choke Bart. The Simpsons all sit on the sofa at the same time and wait for something new to happen.

A Set of Objects, a Situation, a Chain of Events which shall be the Formula of a Particular Emotion; Such that when the External Facts, which must Terminate in Sensory Experience, are Given, the Emotion is Immediately Evoked

1st rule: You do not talk about OBJECTIVE CORRELATIVE.

2nd rule: You DO NOT talk about OBJECTIVE CORRELATIVE.

3rd rule: If someone says "stop" or goes limp or taps out, the OBJECTIVE CORRELATIVE is over.

4th rule: Only two guys to an OBJECTIVE CORRELATIVE.

5th rule: One OBJECTIVE CORRELATIVE at a time.

6th rule: No shirts, no shoes.

7th rule: OBJECTIVE CORRELATIVES will go on as long as they have to.

8th rule: If this is your first night at OBJECTIVE CORRELATIVE, you HAVE to OBJECTIVE CORRELATIVE.

Portions Toll

Turpin came in the shop today and we gee-whizzed for a few minutes before he asked me if the part he ordered last week was in yet. I told him no and explained that the order got placed between catalogs with my vendor, and how was I to know the part would have a new number in the new catalog. He had some words to say about that but he kept it mild because there was a woman in the store with her husband, a couple of newly-weds holding hands, walking the aisles slow, cooling off in the air conditioning. Turpin said Christ Almighty under his breath and then we gee-whizzed again for a few minutes, mostly about his boys, the twins up at State playing football. They're different-looking twins, not identical. But both of them are line-backers. There's been talk in the papers that they both might get drafted by the NFL. He gee-whizzed that too but I could tell he was feeling pretty good about his boys. Then he asked me about my boys. George and Leopold, also twins. Identical. Too identical. And identical also with their mother. Turpin didn't want to ask about George and Leopold. He was just being polite. But since he asked, I gave him a full rundown of their latest nonsense. I told him how they were in the shop last week taking measurements and making sketches. I asked them what they were up to, and George told me they were making

designs for the shop to become a nightclub after my death. Gee-whiz, if he didn't say it like my death was coming soon as Sunday. Now the newlyweds were sitting down on a pair of the collapsible chairs we got on special. The groom bought a cola from the machine and he shared it with his bride. They looked a little too comfortable, like they were waiting for all the hardware and feed to be gone so this place could become a hopping nightspot. Turpin's known for telling the raunchiest jokes you'd ever want to hear, so I gee-whizzed him into telling one, good and loud to hasten the newlyweds' exit. He had a new one about a fellow who figured out a way to get his wife to do that thing that wives don't like to do whenever they took a roadtrip together, right there in the car as he drove. It was a good one. Filthy. Can't remember it to tell it myself, but the punchline was portions toll. It got the newlyweds gone.

Pegs

Diner had a waitress with one leg. Peg was her name.

The short order cook was missing his right arm. His name was Peg, too.

I washed the dishes. Correction: I washed the dirty dishes. Got into a shit-load of trouble my first day on the job when I washed the clean dishes.

I felt a hand on my neck. A sticky hand. It was Sticky, the owner. He's sticky.

"Fucking Sticky," I said.

"Sorry, Peg," he said.

That's right. They call me Peg, too.

My mother was a school nurse. And my father was a hotel detective. And my brother John—fifteen years older than me, still living at home, and skinny, skinny, skinny—was in a band called They Might Be Giants.

I asked my old man if I could get a cool haircut with my dishwashing money.

"Why would you want to go and do that?" he said. His face told me that he was about to say more. I waited a moment, and this is what he said:

"A man with a cool haircut stands out in a crowd. A man who stands out in a crowd has a greater chance of being accused falsely of a crime that he did not commit. Studies—multiple studies—show that so-called eyewitnesses to crimes often connect the crime that they witnessed to the most recent stranger whose appearance was differentiated from that of the standard face in the crowd."

My old man went on to say that he felt the world looming above him now. So different from when he was young. When he was young he felt as if he were standing on top of the world.

"You must feel that way now," he said.

I gave him my best shrug. He sighed like only a hotel detective can sigh. Upstairs, we heard John drop his accordion. I shrugged again and my old man sighed again. He was getting dressed to work the overnight shift at the hotel, which always brings on the sighs. He wears a bellhop uniform as cover. He put on his tasseled fez, red velvet, gold fringe. His fez is tallest among the bellhops.

"Are the other bellhops also hotel detectives?" I asked.

"You kidding me?"

In addition to missing his right arm, Peg the cook has a messed up face. Not all of his facial features face in the same direction. Direct eye contact with Peg the cook is out of the question.

He hollered over from his fry station that I was using too much hot water.

"What's it to you?" I said "It's not like you make the hot water."

Peg called Peg the waitress into the kitchen and they brought me to the utility room. They pointed to the hot water heater.

"Open the hatch," Peg the waitress said.

Inside, dancing within the blue flame, were miniature ver-

sions of both Pegs. At first I thought they were dancing in the flame. But no. They were wrestling one another. The mini Pegs in the flame were whole, no limbs missing. They seemed younger, too. They were really battling. It was impossible to say which Peg was more furious. They appeared to be an equal match.

Narration, Character, Consequence

You are others more sentimental. You are a word-processor. You are a word appliance. You greet each new player as a fool. Deem each new experience a failure.

The receptionist, who stared at her candy cane until she got vertigo, told you she liked your skirt.

For lunch you ate the brand of tuna born in a can.

The telling pause between the sigh and the lie. The hand up your skirt. In the subway.

You should start reading true crime books again.

I like it like that, you told him. But I don't like it like that all the time.

You wrote a dozen poems one semester that your roommate described as dictionary-ish.

Sheila threw fits. So you'd know she was serious. She pointed at the calendar. She said the days are burning. She circled the due date again. Stabbed her marker inside her circle. Bullseye.

Sheila's weekend T-shirt reads: I'm not a negotiator. I'm a bitch.

Sheila has the kind of upper lip that Matt Groening would draw.

He talked with his hands, Stephen. He did emphatic good.

He nodded when he spoke. He nodded when he listened. He wanted to be hypnotized. He said, Hypnotized is an ideal state.

He is balding, but he wears it well. A tall man with a short fuse.

He felt the need to remind you: Fussy gay guys always get their way.

You spent your whole day online and now your face feels as flat as your laptop's screen. You try to smile, to bring an expression to your face, unsure if there's any definition left to your features.

They both remind you that whatever it is you're typing, it must be poetry.

Daring you to be daring.

They got along like a couple of Seventeenth Century British hand-puppets, always fighting, clobbering each other over the head.

Agonized and clear—Dickinson.

Stephen sends you an email: RE Sheila—Power-hungry maniacs do it for the glee.

Not to worry. You have a system of entropy when it comes to words.

You're a little bit winning, you know. Some small part of you is happy. The masochistic part.

Workshop

...In the spirit of respectful observation of National Writers Workshop Day, I am pleased to submit this memorial to Cole Hardy, my first writing teacher. Equal parts gentleman and dope, the man really knew how to make a captive audience deplore him. (He was also a genius at making people feel uncomfortable with their own personal experiences.) He knew not how to impart lessons of craft, and he openly discouraged prose innovation. But, in the end, he was able to reconcile his recondite fears and superstitions into a cogent set of pathologies half-effective (and vain) homilies on writing craft that I have been unable to forget. He said each sentence must be a word camera, snapping a picture of an emotional truth. He said female characters should be named after flowers in first drafts and, if they are still seen to be blooming in the final draft, then they may retain that floral name. He said the best advice his agent of thirty years ever gave him was simply this: Put the bottle down. He called his novels failed short stories, and he said he envied us for our commitment to the truest form of the literary arts. He said that Henry James owed the world an apology. He let his speech become vernacular when he spoke of his mother. He admitted that he was quite a mommy-boy growing up (surprising none of his students). Personification, he said,

was dead. He was aware that he was perceived as pompous, but he said it was a tactical pomposity. He laughed when one of the older women in the workshop said he looked like George H. W. Bush, which he did, though in a chubby way. His hair on top was thin, but he had one dynamic wave that he wet combed to great effect. He owned, by my count, four suits plus one blue blazer and one tweed sportsjacket. He always wore a necktie. He did not own a wristwatch and he was forever asking the class how much time we had left. He never owned a house. He did not drive. He did not like the chairs in our seminar room. He said the chairs in our seminar room were made by a man unfamiliar with human knees. He said a chair is not a chair when it is a weapon. He said he was writing much of his new novel while he dreamt at night. He was surprised that the class was interested in this revelation. He said he'd be happy to tell us how he was doing it, writing his novels while he slept. He said, I am learning my thoughts on the story as I dream. He described it as trying to guide his dreams like a plot to see what he could make happen. He compared the process to making a very specific outline and then projecting the outline in dream form. He said Hemingway was a sheep in wolf's clothing. He said Faulkner was a sheep in wolf's clothing. He said Mailer was a sheep in wolf's clothing. He said Orwell was a sheep in wolf's clothing. He said Camus was a sheep in wolf's clothing. He said Baldwin was a sheep in wolf's clothing. He said Barthelme was a sheep in wolf's clothing. He said Yates was a sheep in wolf's clothing. He said Bukowski was a sheep in wolf's clothing. He said Chuck Palahniuk *is* a sheep in wolf's clothing, and because he was able to pronounce Chuck's last name better than us, nobody in the workshop contradicted him. Sorry, Chuck.

Contemporary Short Story

Nothing funny about lice. Not the first time you get them and not the second. You don't learn anything from lice. There's not a lot to extrapolate. Nothing. And this is the third time I've caught lice. I wonder.

Each time it's been the curse of a stranger. In grammar school it was a girl named Roberta. She was new. She was the first new girl. It was fourth grade in a small town, and we'd never had a new girl before.

Second time was my freshman year at college. A guy named Alan Linde. He only lasted two weeks before he dropped out.

This time I can't be sure. I have a few theories.

I know the cure. The only cure. The shampoo they prescribe will kill the lice and their eggs. But to really get rid of lice, you have to give them to somebody else. You have to pass them on.

They kept telling me to get ready for the party.

"Either wash your hair or put a cap on," Mark Allen said.

I was having trouble lifting myself from the couch. My head was burning. And itching.

Then people started appearing. People we know. Friends.

Tina. Joel. Sue and Ann. They came together. Then there were more people, singles arriving in dribs and drabs. Roger. Rob. Timmy Mayhew. Jennifer.

They were guests arriving. The party was at our place.

Nobody told me.

It was in honor of our latest fourth housemate, Jeff Hector. A magazine in Wyoming that's been publishing his short stories had decided to devote an entire issue to him. Good for him.

I'll say it now: I don't like Jeff Hector.

Things haven't been going good for me since he moved in three months ago. He serves his purpose. He fills the extra room. He pays his rent. But something's wrong about him.

He leaves the apartment three times a day, and comes back with his food. He makes fast to his room. He eats at his desk. Mostly he gets soup. He's big on soup. He's a soup man. And he slurps his soup. I hear him in his room, slurping his soup.

His typing is non-stop. He's got an old IBM electric type-writer that whirrs loud when he switches it on. It's big. It makes a banging noise with each letter typed, and the little desk he keeps it on squeaks every time the carriage returns.

His fiction, which I've yet to read, has been characterized by both Mark and Gerald Allen as belonging to the loner-guy genre. He's got one about a loner-guy traveling. One about a loner-guy thinking about traveling. One about a loner-guy who just finished traveling.

And he can't piss straight. Since he's moved in there's piss on the floor beside the hopper and on the rim. That's not good.

I was always a sensitive boy. I'm not digressing. I feel it's important to get that out. I always wanted to be a writer. I used to watch *The Waltons* every Thursday night to see John Boy Walton sitting at his desk at the end of the show, writing a story about his family in his tablet.

That's what a young writer should be like, John Boy Walton. I don't have a tablet. I bounce around on my computer, switching screens from one incomplete story to another. Fixing things. Adding things. Deleting things.

Jeff Hector closes the door behind him, sits at his little desk and types away. He writes without a shirt on, bare-chested. If he gets stuck, which is rare, he paces the room, lifting his weights.

As I predicted, Jeff Hector didn't show for his party. I tried to get some resentment brewing when it became apparent that he wasn't coming. But no dice. Everybody's having too much fun, and some of them seem to actually like him.

Gerald Allen begins proposing a toast to Jeff Hector, which I felt compelled to interrupt.

"To hell with Jeff Hector," I said. "He doesn't deserve a party. I'm not celebrating him. We're all writers here. Practitioners of the contemporary short story. Let's just celebrate the contemporary short story."

I am literally booed.

Then a rhythmic clapping begins. And then a chant of Jeff Hector's last name. "Hec-tor. Hec-tor. Hec-tor."

Around midnight I discovered that if I wore my cap backwards, catcher's style, my head itched less. And when I stayed still, the lice moved less. So I wedged myself between the refrigerator and the kitchen table. I could see the party fine, and I could talk to people when they came for beer.

The truth is I was looking for someone to give the lice to. Of course, everybody knew I had the lice and they were ostracizing me.

When Missy Dean came into the kitchen to visit me, I

stopped thinking about my lice. And Jeff Hector.

Missy is taking the semester off for financial reasons. She's working as a nanny for a lesbian couple who had babies at the same time, nine days apart. The babies have the same father, an anonymous donor. The babies, two boys, have the same father. They are related by blood, half brothers.

Missy pointed at my backwards cap. "Hey," she said. "Johnny Bench."

She snatched the cap off my head and put it on before I could stop her.

Requited

Visiting my grandfather in the hospital. He just had surgery to replace his artificial hips. That's right. He's eighty-two years old, and he just got his second set of artificial hips installed.

"Gramps," I ask him. "What is it with you and hips?"

"Too much screwin'," he says.

It's true. The man has had a busy sex life. Hundreds of women. Maybe more than a thousand. When Gramps retired, he burned through his 401k with a month of lapdances at the Foxy Lady. He's like that.

"You take it easy with these new hips," I say. "Leave the ladies alone."

Gramps nods in the direction of the nurse tending to his roommates. Gramps makes a clicking sound with his false teeth and winks.

"No," I say.

Gramps says, "Yup. Last night after my sponge bath."

Grandma looks up from her knitting. She considers the nurse, a stocky woman with a gray buzzcut—the drill sergeant type—in her early fifties. Grandma says, "Yup."

My grandparents divorced about forty years ago. They've rec-

onciled a few times over the years, never for more than a month or two, but more frequently in the past few years.

My grandmother always has a smile on her face. She's had no other man in her life besides Gramps and she seems to be happy about that. She likes to knit sweaters for everybody, she likes to sew quilts, she likes to read thick books from the library, and she likes to watch weepy old movies.

I ask her why she put up with Gramps all these years. She tells me she's never let him get the better of her. She says she's in charge, but she lets him stick around because she has a soft spot for the old fool.

Grandma says, "One time I came home and caught him sound asleep in our bed with one of his ladies. I hustled her out of the bed, careful not to wake him. Then I sewed the blanket to the bedspread with him stuck inside. Got a broom from the kitchen and beat him with the handle."

"Actually, Grandma, that's something that one of Willie Nelson's wives did to him."

"Shit," says Grandma. "You sure about that?"

Walking the shiny halls of the hospital with Gramps.

"Look at this, Peter."

I turn to see Gramps swiveling his hips, hula style. It was a bit obscene.

"These new hips are going to suit me just fine," he says. "You should get yourself a pair."

"I plan to get a lifetime out of the original set that God gave me," I say.

"You ought to be out there screwing through those hips," he says. "Break your hips, not your heart."

Our walk takes us outside, into a shady courtyard. Gramps speaks my ex-wife's name. Since we're outside, I spit on the ground, just to get a laugh out of Gramps.

"I had a wife but couldn't keep her," I say. "She wanted babies, and I couldn't give her any."

Gramps says, "Then you go find a woman who wants what you can give her."

I make a remark about what he's given my grandmother over the years—heartache.

"Your grandmother isn't as innocent as she seems," says Gramps.

"Oh, is that right?"

"Once, she had relations with a man she knew to have syphilis just so she could pass it on to me!"

"Actually, Gramps, that's something that Hillary Clinton did to Bill back when he was Governor of Arkansas."

"You sure about that?"

I pick up Gramps when he's discharged from the hospital the next day.

"Where to?" I ask him.

"Your grandmother's place."

"What about your nurse?"

He makes a sour face, says an expletive quietly. "I could move in with her so long as I resigned myself to a lifetime of foreplay consisting of me moving my bowels in a bedpan and then submitting to a rough sponge bath. That's not for me."

"Enough."

Gramps says I could take him to Grace Herot's house. "If I only knew where she lived today."

"Is she your one unrequited love, Gramps?"

"Hell," says Gramps. "I requited Grace Herot. I requited her a dozen times the summer we were sixteen."

He goes on to name a few places where he and Grace did their requiting. Then he suddenly begins crying. I think the tears are for Grace Herot. But no. Gramps has fallen in love

with my Grandmother again.

"I'm dedicating these new hips to your grandmother," he says.

Calendar Sisters

April is the cruelest girl. June, her younger sister, is, somehow, meaner. May, in the middle, is sweet, sweet, sweet. Oh, May. April. June. May. The Calendar sisters. April shakes her head no. April is a don't, a won't, and a never mind. April says, Not now. April won't say when. April says, Stop asking. April wants to stay at home. April says, Don't call during dinner. April says, Do this and do that. April says, June is coming into her curves. June says, I want to go to the beach. June wants a bigger beach towel but a smaller swimsuit. June is working on a new kind of smile. June tells you to bring your camera. June says, Why am I so blurry? June says, I should be in the center. June says, You made me look like May in this one. June says, Delete them all but send the last one to May. With May, everything is permissible. Yes is May's word. Yes is May's policy. May says, Yes prevents unhappiness. May says, Why not. May says, Yes, you can. May, May, May. Oh, May, May, May. Yes, you May.

Direct Address

We're the homely couple that just moved in down the hall, John and Ellen Pratt. You said hello to us in the hallway last Sunday and then again this Wednesday. You're a very handsome couple.

This is an awkward approach, we realize, but we'd like to be friends with you. We had intended to wait until you approached us, but we know you're busy people with hectic schedules—last Saturday we counted, and your car was in and out of its space seven times.

We'd like you to know that we've had successful relationships with other good-looking couples, and we wouldn't mind if we were on your B-list. We even realize you might not want to have a public relationship with us, and we understand that. We imagine that an evening of dinner and drinks and a rented movie would be wonderful. That's an invitation for your next free Friday night. You tell us.

What we'd really like is to hear the story of how you first met. We're good listeners. We have big ears, and we feel certain that your story will be interesting.

Our story is interesting, we think. We met at a sleep research seminar. We were guinea pigs. Our cots were next-door. We were hooked up to a network of computers that recorded

our brain activity while we slept. We were both in graduate school at the time, and we did it for the money.

After the second night, an attendant discovered that our data was a perfect match. The print-outs that tracked our sleep and dream patterns could be laid one on top of the other and be seen as one line.

We became the focus of the study. We were a bona fide phenomenon, and night after night our sleep/dream data were exactly the same, identical. Though they weren't sure what their findings meant, they were becoming very excited about us—just as we were becoming very excited about each other. They asked us if we would consider sleeping in the same bed one night, just to see how our brain activity would be affected. We were shy about it, but we consented.

That first night we spent in the same bed together a sleep communication was discovered. We spoke to one another in a very formal, courtly manner, characterized by a comically exaggerated politeness. Without fail, we used direct address each time we spoke to one another. It was really very funny. While listening to the audio tape of that night, we fell in love.

We excused ourselves from the experiment in order to pursue the research on our own, and we have not slept apart since. Our marriage is our research. Which is what we've been doing, off and on, for the past nine years. We're book editors, and we've been working on a book about couples who have communication abilities that go beyond what is considered to be the norm. We've conducted more than five thousand interviews with couples around the world who have experienced many different types of hyper-communication abilities. Our research is anecdotal, not scientific. But we have what we feel are very definitive findings.

We have discovered that nearly all of the responding couples also have a shared negative characteristic that, in almost every case, defines their relationship to the rest of the world.

We've documented alcoholic couples. Mentally challenged couples. HIV-positive couples. Interracial couples. Obese couples. Couples who have been unable to consummate their relationship. Dwarf couples. Insomniac couples. Wheelchair couples. Toothless couples. A deaf couple whose signing has multiplied the manual alphabet tenfold. Epistolary couples. Infertile couples. Cancer couples. Aphasiac couples. Illiterate couples. Alzheimer couples. Heroin couples. Prison couples. Webbed-footed couples. Suicidal couples. Homeless couples. Blind couples. UFO couples. Acne couples. Hypochondriac couples. And a good number of homely couples, like us.

We have a very strong feeling that you might be such a couple—hyper-communicative. We apologize if it bothers you that we believe your successful relationship might be centered on a shared negative characteristic. We are curious about you as a couple. We want to know how such a handsome man and woman communicate. We can't imagine that either of you have a single negative characteristic, let alone share one. But maybe…

This is a serious inquiry.

Rosencrantz and Guildenstern
Are Wed

Arm in arm, Rosencrantz (hereafter ROSE*) and Guildenstern (hereafter* GIL*) enter a tiny, simple chapel and face an empty altar. They are well dressed. They are well groomed. They are confused. They are in good spirits, despite all.*

ROSE: Why are we waiting?

GIL: That is the question?

ROSE: What are we waiting for?

GIL: That is another question?

ROSE: *(Reaches deep into his coat pocket, pulls out a large coin. He flips the coin, calls it midair.)*: Heads.

GIL: That's seventy-eight in a row.

ROSE: This coin has two heads.

GIL: We have two heads.

ROSE: Do you remember that deck of cards?

GIL: I do. Clean-shaven Kings. Bearded Queens.

ROSE: And all those Jacks! Forty-four Jacks! *(Flips coin again.)*

ROSE and GIL *(Together.)*: Heads.

ROSE and GIL *(Forgetting the coin, together)*: Jinx!

GIL: Please insert another quarter. The jinx machine is out of order.

ROSE *(Checks his wristwatch.)*: Many people are late today.

GIL: We are people. We are on time.

ROSE: The invitations?

GIL: Mailed months ago.

ROSE: The RSVPs?

GIL: Received. Only a few came with regrets.

ROSE: The protesters outside came early.

GIL: They had to fashion signs.

ROSE: Everything is a sign.

GIL: Everything is fashion.

ROSE: Except those dear protesters.

GIL: (*Checks his wristwatch.*): This is very much like a play.

ROSE: Everything is play. We earn no wages.

GIL: Marriage is a play.

ROSE: Marriage is an errand.

GIL: The Judge said it was the most reasonable ransom note he'd ever read.

ROSE: It was a license for marriage that we both did sign.

GIL: True that.

ROSE: And you have the rings?

GIL: You mean nooses.

ROSE: That's a borrowed cliché.

GIL (*Clears his throat to deliver his line.*): Borrowing dulls the edge of husbandry.

ROSE: That is not your line.

GIL: Something old. Something new. Something borrowed. Something blue.

ROSE: Are we here?

GIL: (*Makes no reply.*)

ROSE: Am I talking to myself?

GIL: You are talking to myself.

ROSE: Is it not today?

GIL: And do you, Rosencrantz, take me, Guildenstern?

ROSE: I have taken you many times, and you have took me.

GIL: But here, in this church, will you take me?

They are interrupted by a church bell.

ROSE: Do you hear that?

GIL: I do not hear a bell, if that's what you're asking.

ROSE: Oh, well. If you must marry, marry a fool.

GIL: Who said that?

ROSE: I said that.

GIL: But you did not say it first.

ROSE: I did not hear it repeated. Did I say it twice?

GIL: I say, We will have no more marriages.

ROSE: We will have ours.

GIL: We have had ours.

Simultaneously, they look at their hands and see that they are wearing wedding bands.

ROSE: Marriage means mischief.

GIL: Marriage means tragedy.

ROSE: Tragedy. Comedy. History. Pastoral. Pastoral-comical. Historical-pastoral.

GIL: Urban hip-hop sit-com. Agit-prop rom-com. *Lifetime* docu-drama.
ABC Afterschool Special.

ROSE: Tragical-historical. Tragical-comical-historical-pastoral, scene individable.

GIL: Neo-noir. Retro-grindhouse. Chickflick. Arthouse sci-fi. Spaghetti western.

ROSE: A poem unlimited. Marriage cannot be too heavy, nor can it be too light.

GIL: You can't be too rich and you can't be too thin.

ROSE: For the law of wit and the liberty, these are the only men.

GIL: We are the only men…here.

ROSE: And I already know the sequel to this our wedding day.

GIL: I know it too. But what shall we call it?

ROSE: *Rosencrantz and Guildenstern Are Dads*!

Boy Toat

Toy boat toy boat boy toat boy toat boy toat boy...

Toy boat toy boat toy boat toy boat toy boat toy boat toy boat toy boat toy boat toy boat toy boat toy boat toy boat toy boat toy boat toy boat toy boat toy boat boy toat boy toat boy toat boy...

Toy boat toy boat toy boat toy boat toy boat toy boat toy boat toy boat toy boat toy boat toy boat boat toy boat boy toat boy toat boy toat boy...

Toy boat toy boat toy boat toy boat toy boat toy boat boy toat boy toat boy toat boy...

Toy boat toy boat boy toat boy toat boy toat boy...

Toy boat toy boat boy toat boy toat boy...

Boy toat boy

toat boy toat. Boy toat.

Chaos

Here comes Cheryl with a box.

"What's in the box, Cheryl?"

"It's not a box."

Cheryl has a history with boxes.

Once, she put all the pieces to all of our boardgames into one big box. The Game of Life. Boggle. Yahtzee. Jenga. Connect Four. Trivial Pursuit. Apples-to-Apples. Sorry. Monopoly, of course. Even a few oldies like Chutes and Ladders and Candy Land. And everything that was inside dad's backgammon briefcase. She wrecked game night.

"Just by saying it's not a box doesn't mean it's not a box."

"It's not a box."

Mom says Cheryl has a natural disposition for Zen. She says that I tend toward chaos. I think she has that backwards.

"If it's not a box, what do you call it?"

"It's a container."

"What's inside?"

"Nothing. This is the box that I am going to keep empty."

"Cheryl."

"What?"

"You just called your container a box."

Cheryl laughs.

I touch a finger to my chin and look up at the ceiling.

Cheryl asks me what I'm thinking about.

"I'm thinking of all the things I will put inside your empty box."

Sibella

"Your shirt don't get along with your pants," she tells me.

Thick accent. Thin lips. Hair a blond pile atop a narrow face. Arms blue with tattoos, like toile, from her slender wrists to her lovely shoulders. Plus a major tattoo on her left hip, visible when she removes her leather jacket: a sideways scene of a pirate swinging from a broken mast.

"The expression you're looking for," I say, "is 'go with.' My shirt doesn't go with my pants."

Her history is familiar to me. When she first got into the art biz, she slept with the collectors. These days she sleeps with painters. She takes me to her condo, kicks off her cowboy boots. Her feet are a mess. She has the equivalent of five big toes on each foot. No. Five big toes on each foot that have been crushed flat.

"This is what dancing pretty does to your feet," she explains.

She'd spent her earliest years on point. Spinning her toes big and flat.

She dances for me. No music in her under-furnished condo, but she dances like an angel. Rife with eros, she is.

By morning, she had me signed to her agency. Over lunch, she sells three of my shittiest canvasses to a youthful investment banker. Her tits are that good.

I have a reputation for being the best behaved artist in New York City. I am punctual. I am polite. Sincere. I write timely thank you notes. I behave at parties. I am respectful to those deserving my respect, and I avoid those who are not. I am generous when I am flush. I repay loans.

I am productive and an effective networker. I work eight to ten hours a day in the studio or en plein air. I pay my models triple scale for long sessions, and I do not try to seduce them. Though I am still a young painter, I mentor those just starting out, guiding them through the museums and bringing them along to the right galleries.

Many of my colleagues warn me against working with Sibella. I tell them she is good to me, that she is good for my work.

She buys me clothes and gets my hair restyled. She gets me to the gym. She sells my work.

She has three lethal dimples, two on her left cheek and one high on the right cheek. Her teeth are fierce. Her eyes are too. She has a movie star's control of her gestures. She smells like a yoga mat.

I ask her, "That first night we were together. Did you slip something into my drink? A drug to enhance my performance?"

She dismisses the question, brings me a small cup of weak tea at midnight and lures me to her bed.

I call her to my studio to show her a few new paintings. Bigger canvases, as she'd asked. But she is underwhelmed.

"Why so dainty?"

She wants to know why my new work is so dainty. I feel I could cry. I take her in an embrace and lead her toward the bed that I keep in the back of the studio.

She pulls away from me. "Don't hide behind your erection," she says.

"I want to paint you."

"No," she says, offering no reason.

"If I can't paint you, I won't paint."

"Suit yourself."

"If you leave me, I'll paint you anyway and I will paint you hellish."

"I can sell hellish," she says.

She reminds me of the terms of our contract. I want to ask her where she has been for the last three weeks. I want to know why she ignores my texts and voicemail messages.

I break the paint brush in my hand and then a dozen more that are within my reach.

She claps her hands. "More," she says.

I punch my fist through a wet canvas, throw it at the wall.

Her clapping becomes rhythmic. "More! More! More!" She is chanting.

I break all my brushes, snap every one of them. I stomp on my fresh paint tubes. I mean business.

She stops her clapping and goes silent for a moment. She takes pictures of my demolished studio with her cellphone.

"You've done well," she says.

I feel ashamed. I make a mental tally of paints wasted, the brushes and canvases.

She begins to undress. "I want you to paint me hellish," she says.

DOB/RIP

1. DOB, SSN, 4H, FFA, DDT, RIP

2. DOB, SSN, BSA, ROTC, USMC, SNAFU, AWOL, PTSD, ASBO, AA, SSI, SSDI, VHA, DNR, RIP

3. DOB, SSN, UFO, UFO, UFO, UFO, UFO, UFO, UFO, UFO, UFO, UFO, UFO, UFO, UFO, UFO, UFO, UFO, UFO, SGW, RIP

4. DOB, SSN, SAT, MIT, GRE, MIT, PhD, LSD, DJ, E, H, OD, RIP

5. DOB, SSN, GSA, SAT, UCONN, NCAA, WNBA, DAR, USS, M&M's, DD, BK, DQ, PHF, HP, HFCS, NIDDM, RIP

6. DOB, SSN, QB, HGH, GBP, HGH, AS, NYJ, MV, RIP

7. DOB, SSN, CPA, DEB, ADL, IRS, JOW, RIP

8. DOB, SSN, EGBDF, R&R, LP, MTV, CD, NARAS, GUMP, CL/NS, RIP

9. DOB, SSN, IBM PC, MS-DOS, SQL, WYSIWIG, HTML, CSS, MOB, HIV, AIDS, RIP

10. DOB, APGAR, RIP

KEY

....

AA: Alcoholics Anonymous
APGAR: Appearance, Pulse, Grimace, Activity, Respiration
AAS: Anabolic-Androgenic Steroid
ADL: Arthur D. Little
AIDS: Acquired Immune Deficiency Syndrome
ASBO: Anti-Social Behavior Disorder
AWOL: Absent Without Leave
BSA: Boys Scouts of America
BK: Burger King
CD: Compact Disc
CL/NS Crash Landing/No Survivors
CPA: Certified Public Accountant
CSS: Cascading Style Sheets
DAR: Daughters of the American Revolution
DD: Dunkin' Donuts
DDT: Dichlorodiphenyltrichloroethane
DEB: Double-Entry Bookkeeping
DJ: Disk Jockey
DNR: Do Not Resuscitate
DOB: Date of Birth
DQ: Dairy Queen
E: Ecstasy
EGBDF: Every Good Boy Deserves Fudge
FBI: Federal Bureau of Investigations
FFA: Future Farmers of America

GBP: Green Bay Packers

GRE: Graduate Record Examinations

GSA: Girl Scouts of America

GUMP: Gas, Undercarriage, Mixture, Propeller

H: Heroin

HFCS: High-Fructose Corn Syrup

HGH: Human Growth Hormone

HIV: Human Immunodeficiency Virus

HP: Hot Pockets

HTML: HyperText Markup Language

IBM PC: International Business Machines Personal Computer

IRS: Internal Revenue Service

JOW: Jumped Out Window

LP: Long-playing (record album)

LSD: Lysergic Acid Diethylamide

MIT: Massachusetts Institute of Technology

MOB: Mail Order Bride

MS-DOS: MicroSoft Disk Operating System

M&M's: Mars & Murrie

MV: Minnesota Vikings

MTV: Music Television

NAACP: National Association for the Advancement of Colored People

NCAA: National Collegiate Athletic Association

NIDDM: Non-Insulin-Dependent Diabetes Mellitus

NYJ: New York Jets

NARAS: National Academy of Recording Arts and Sciences

OD: Overdose

PhD: Doctor of Philosophy

PHF: Potentially Hazardous Food

PTSD: Post-Traumatic Stress Disorder

QB: Quarterback

RIP: Rest in Peace

R&R: Rock 'n' Roll

SAT: Scholastic Aptitude Test
SGW: Self-inflicted Gunshot Wound
SNAFU: Situation Normal, All Fucked Up
SSDI: Supplemental Security Disability Insurance
SSI: Supplemental Security Insurance
SSN: Social Security Number
UCONN: University of Connecticut
USMC: United States Marine Corps
UFO: Unidentified Flying Object
USS: United States Senator
VHA: Veterans Health Administration
WNBA: Women's National Basketball Association
WYSIWIG: What You See Is What You Get
4H: Head Heart Hands Health

Gallop

The phone is ringing. You pick up your coffee mug and put it to your ear. Hello. Hot coffee spills into your ear. You throw the coffee mug across the room. The phone is ringing. Hello. You stand and touch the ceiling. The ceiling is eight feet high. You are seven feet two inches tall. The phone is ringing. Hello. When you were born you weighed in at seventeen pounds and nine ounces. You had front teeth and long hair down your neck. The phone is ringing. Hello. You touch the ceiling again and stare at the marks your hands have made on the ceiling. You hate the ceiling. You punch the ceiling. The phone is ringing. Hello. You punch the walls. Decorative plates fall to the floor. The phone is ringing. Hello. You punch the ceiling again and your fist goes through, into the apartment above. The woman upstairs screams. Help. The phone is ringing. Hello. The woman upstairs falls through the hole in the ceiling and she lands in your arms. Her screaming is in your ears. Help. The phone is ringing. Hello. The woman upstairs slaps at your face, pulls on your ears. The phone is ringing. Hello. When you were a boy, you galloped in your grandfather's fields with his ponies. You bit at their tails and grandfather slapped you. The phone is ringing. Hello. The woman has climbed out of your arms and has saddled herself on your shoulders. Help.

The phone is ringing. Hello. The woman is reaching her arms into her apartment, through the hole in the ceiling. You want to let her go but you hold onto her tightly with one hand and with the other you pull at the pipes and wiring exposed in the ceiling. Now water and sparks. The phone is still ringing. Hello. A broken steam pipe whistles. The woman from upstairs is biting your back. Help. You are running in place. You hear a snort from your nose when you inhale. Your lips make a blubbering sound when you exhale. The woman upstairs is bouncing on your shoulders. You wish she would laugh and enjoy the ride. But she screams again. Help. The phone is ringing. Hello.

Twin Thing

My twin called this morning to ask what I was wearing.

"Seriously?"

"I need to know."

We're forty-three. He just can't give it up.

My brother is deeply into twin lore. Twinness has been his obsession since birth. He reads every book on twins that comes out, even the scholarly studies and the coffee table photo books of twin faces. He tells me what the birth of twins signifies in African cultures, how twins are revered in Japan. He understands my unease with being a twin, but he can't help himself.

"Twins separated at birth grow up to be more alike that twins raised together in the same home," he told me once.

I rebelled against dressing identically at a young age. I would strip off any and all matching outfits. My mother would fall into tears whenever I did this. It was such a struggle for her to get two young boys dressed, and there I was disrobing immediately.

And, making matters worse, my brother would follow suit and take off his clothes, too. He wasn't rebelling against parad-

ing around town in matching attire. He was just doing what he always did: copying everything that I did.

One day I refused to speak. We must have been ten or so. Our parents and older sisters were amused, but my brother was not.

"I'll get him to say something," my brother said. "He'll talk to me."

But I wouldn't. No matter what he did. No matter how hard he tried. I wouldn't speak.

Finally, he said, "I get it. I get it. Mute twin."

Our parents died about six months apart, when my brother and I were thirty-two. I came home for their services, and both times my brother tried to convince me to move back home, to live with him in his condo. He was worried for me, he said. He wanted me to settle down, stop working in nightclubs, moving from one city to the next. He asked me if I mixed myself an identical drink for every one that I served when I was tending bar.

That's right. I'm the alchy twin. I'm the twin with the purple nose.

After he got married, my brother doubled his efforts to keep in touch with me, despite my frequent moves. My brother married a twin, Crystal, and they have no children. They've been on the wait list for some time to adopt twins from China.

I made the mistake of giving him my cell number and he called me every few days, always asking me if I had just been thinking of him. He believed that our thoughts were synchronous. When he thought of me, I must be thinking of him, and vice-versa.

He was so lonely, he said. "I really miss you, brother."

I once briefly dated a twin, myself. Her name was Denise. Her twin was a brother. His name? You guessed: Dennis. He was a bit of a crossdresser, she told me.

"Mostly he dresses as a woman to do karaoke," she said. "I'm telling you now so you don't get freaked out if you see a six-foot version of me walk into your bar some night."

This is the moment I should have told Denise that I was also a twin. But I didn't. I quit my job at the club and got a bus ticket to Las Vegas.

When I was in rehab for the third time in two years (court-ordered), my brother sent me a new suit so I would look my best when I checked out. Like the Minnesota Twins cap he had sent me years ago and all of the souvenir T-shirts he had air-mailed to me from his travels, I knew that the suit's twin hung in his closet and that he would be wearing the suit, a thousand miles away, on the day of my discharge.

For me, being a twin feels like living between French mirrors, trapped in deep, endless reflections. For my brother, being a twin—he said to me once—feels like having four legs on the ground. Like no wind could knock him over.

My brother's communication with me now is a tolerable few emails a week, mostly forwarded items about twins in the news. Some I read and some I delete as soon as I see his favorite subject line: Twin Thing.

But there was something too urgent in his call this morning—asking me what I was wearing. I had the feeling that he was ramping up to come at me hard one more time to move

back home, to live within his reach.

"I think about you all the time," he said before I hung up on him.

Later, as I finished my last drink before I left for work, I typed the message quickly and didn't have a second thought before I hit send: By the time you read this, I will be dead. Brother, I am sorry. But tonight I am going to kill myself.

My Secret Brand

My secret brand whistles three notes. My secret brand is a recognized leader in the market. My secret brand is avuncular and auntabulous. My secret brand has been working on a train story ever since Johnny Cash passed. My secret brand is task-focused and goal-oriented. My secret brand has a density that is off the charts. My secret brand decries corporate irredentism. My secret brand laughs when it says glow sticks. My secret brand will date your sister—even the sister that no other brand will date. My secret brand is fomenting public disbelief in its competitor's claims. My secret brand owns two-thirds of the market share. My secret brand told you that joke a few years ago that you keep telling yourself. My secret brand is like the Blue Man Group without any makeup or messy props. My secret brand is flexible on grammar, usage, and punctuation as long as the error benefits voice. My secret brand considers the sun but does not stare at it. My secret brand is no longer carbonated. My secret brand will hold a grudge for a maximum of seven years. My secret brand is taking a little break. No biggie. My secret brand can make any space habitable. My secret brand says yes to fried clams and pink lemonade. My secret brand has engineered great comebacks in the past and has a history of falling up. My secret brand is all about Saturday afternoon. My secret

brand is tall. Taller than NBA tall. Taller than storybook tall. Taller than fee-fie-foe-fum tall. My secret brand is wide. I won't say how wide exactly or offer here any similes of wideness. My secret brand seeks strategic partnerships that are mutually rewarding. My secret brand is all the way live. My secret brand can dunk, sure, but my secret brand just goes in for the layup. My secret brand has a flannel tongue, a vibram sole, a steel toe, and unbreakable laces. My secret brand is defined by its tastes, some illegal and others harmful to the soul. My secret brand is a stack of old notebooks, their margins doodled to death. My secret brand eats when it's hungry and drinks when it's dry. My secret brand asks only for your disposable income. My secret brand appreciates your loyalty. My secret brand is all over me. All over me.

Chick Magnet

I have a chick magnet. I bought it online. $9.95. Came in the mail last week.

First time I use it, it works like a charm. I put the chick magnet in my right front pants pocket, as instructed in the user's manual, and approach a pretty woman I've seen standing on the street corner near my apartment almost every day for the past several months. She's on the corner in the morning when I leave for work. She's on the corner in the afternoon when I walk home for lunch. And she's on the corner at dinnertime, too, and late into the evening. I walk by frequently and she always returns my smile. Sometimes I walk by even when I have no place to go, like on the weekends.

Her name, I know, is DeeDee. She always wears short skirts and tight tops. She also wears pretty shoes that have clear high heels, which, from a distance, make it appear like she is floating just a few inches off the ground. And she has the cutest walk—she takes these short happy marching steps.

I've wanted to speak to DeeDee for the longest time. I have seen many men approach her, and she is always receptive and friendly. I am nervous, like I'm always nervous when I ask a woman out, but knowing the chick magnet is in my pocket gives me confidence.

"I was wondering," I begin, "if you might like to go out on a…"

"Date?" DeeDee says the hardest word for me.

"Yes," I say happily. "A date."

She accepts quickly and reaches out to take my hand.

"My friend has a car right over there," she says, pointing to a well-maintained, bronze Chrysler 300.

In the back seat of her friend's car, DeeDee is very affectionate. Immediately. She takes off her top without my even asking. The date ends quickly but DeeDee seems to be as satisfied as me.

"Can I have forty dollars?" she says.

I feel guilty that I haven't taken her to dinner or even for a cup of coffee. I give her two twenties. "Do you want to see me again?" DeeDee asks, folding the twenties into her tiny pink purse.

"Of course," I say, not even trying to hide my infatuation.

I stick the chick magnet to my fridge and study her closely. She is about three inches tall. She is a bendable magnetic statue of a curvy woman with no clothes on. She has a layer of rubbery flesh that is both firm and soft. The chick magnet's face is old-fashioned pretty, and she has wavy blond hair. If real women were the size of my chick magnet, men would eat them. The chick magnet's feet have a stronger magnetic charge than her head. She sticks to the fridge well enough, but gravity, in the form of her big rubber hair and big rubber breasts, causes her to slowly slip into a legs up position.

My next two dates with DeeDee are nearly identical to the first, in the backseat of her friend's Chrysler 300. I'm comfortable inside Chrysler 300s because my mother and both of my

aunts drive Chrysler 300s. By our third date, DeeDee seems to be going through the motions. She asks me for the forty dollars as soon as we get into the car.

I don't mind the forty dollars every time we go on a date. I don't mind DeeDee's narrow definition of a date. Forty dollars is really no more than I would have spent on her if she were the kind of girlfriend who liked to get flowers every once in a while. She's my girlfriend and I'm happy to give the money to her.

Friendly, yes, but Dee Dee is not a pushover. One time I saw DeeDee get into an argument on the corner with another young woman. Their dispute seemed to be about who got to the corner first that day. DeeDee slapped the other woman right across the face, and I thought that would be the end of that. But DeeDee continued to slap the woman even after the woman had fallen to the ground. Then Dee Dee pulled the woman to her feet by her hair and gave her quite a push to get her on her way.

I work as a scheduling coordinator at a free law clinic. I schedule appointments, reschedule appointments, and cancel appointments. The attorneys cancel more appointments than the criminals. I should say that some of the clients are not criminals—I hate being cynical.

I have a crush on one of the attorneys, Miranda Lopez. She's about forty, but she dresses like she's seventeen. I've heard the other attorneys around the office say that she isn't a very good attorney. I believe this is true. We have a party in the office every time one of the attorneys wins a case. We've never had a party to celebrate one of Miranda's cases. Still, she has a very sunny disposition. And wonderfully white teeth.

The more I look at the chick magnet, the more I see her resemblance to DeeDee. This must be why the chick magnet doesn't seem to work with other women. Not like it works with DeeDee.

I send an email to the manufacturer to ask if they have plans to market other models of the chick magnet, perhaps a chick magnet who has dark hair with short bangs and who isn't so buxom but who is trim and Hispanic. The manufacturer of the chick magnet does not respond to my email.

Much as I like DeeDee, it is clear to me that she does not see our relationship as exclusive. It's obvious that she is not looking for a long-term commitment, and I know that she is seeing other men—I see her seeing other men in the Chrysler 300.

I take the chick magnet off the fridge and use a black magic marker to change her hair color. I use some of my mother's makeup to darken the chick magnet's complexion. There is little I can do to reduce the size of her breasts, but when I pinch the chick magnet's back, the chest flattens a bit in the front. I place the remodeled chick magnet in my right front pants pocket and begin to think of things to say to Miranda when I get to the office.

But as I step out the door, I see Miranda standing on the corner—DeeDee's corner—speaking with the woman DeeDee had been unfriendly with. I freeze in my shoes, but Miranda sees me and calls out my name. She waves me over, and introduces me to her client. Her name is Jennifer and she has bruises on her eyes and cuts on her chin.

Jennifer shakes my hand and says, "I spoke with you on the phone yesterday. When I made this appointment."

Miranda smiles at me and I smile back. She is going to win this case.

Seven Personifications

One—The umbrella stands in the bin beside the front door, thirsty for rain.

Two—The pool sees each child as a sponge.

Three—The pond thinks of herself as a little lake.

Four—The watercooler doesn't like to fill big glasses, preferring the tiny disposable cone cups.

Five—The bathtub refuses to drain.

Six—The ocean spits at the big houses that sit on its shore and sighs at the seagulls.

Seven—The fire hydrant closes its eyes and waits for the dog to finish.

Emily Dickison As If

From *The Collected Poems of Emily Dickinson*

When morning comes, it is as if a hundred drums did round my pillow roll, as if my brain had split, with specimens of song, as if for you to choose, as if a chirping brook upon a toilsome way set bleeding feet to minuets without the knowing why, as if a bobolink, carolled and mused and carolled, then bubbled slow away, as if no sail the solstice passed that maketh all things new.

I feel as if the grass were pleased to have it intermit, it sounded as if the streets were running, and then the streets stood still, as if some caravan of sound on deserts, in the sky, had broken rank, as if a duchess pass!

There came one drop of giant rain, as if the hands that held the dams had parted hold, as if it held but the might of a child, as if the resurrection were nothing very odd!

At morning in a truffled hut it stops upon a spot as if it tarried always—as if the house were his, as if it were his own! As if some little Arctic flower, upon the polar hem, went wandering down the latitudes, as if this little flower to Eden wandered in, so gay a flower bereaved the mind as if it were a woe, as if

the cloud that instant slit and let the fire through, as numb to revelation as if my trade were bone.

I'm different from before, as if I breathed superior air, as if my life were shaven and fitted to a frame, as if the chart were given, as if a kingdom cared!

Mothers, a Drabble

My mother and your mother were out hanging clothes. My mother asked your mother why were both of their husbands such louses. Your mother suggested to my mother that they should be each other's spouses. My mother confessed to your mother that she had once kissed a girl when she was an undergraduate. Your mother told my mother that she was an out and out LUG when she was an undergraduate. My mother whispered something into your mother's ear. Your mother giggled at whatever it was that my mother whispered. Your mother kissed my mother right on the mouth. Mothers.

Comfort Food

Gabby and Morgan meet for lunch every Friday afternoon. Today they're at Golden Brown, a new homestyle restaurant in town.

"I love these menus," Gabby says. "Pictures."

"I don't love our waitress," Morgan says. "She is not fat enough."

"She's got foster mother written all over her."

"Maybe she'll adopt us. After lunch."

They examine their menus in silence. Twice Gabby tells the waitress they need more time. The waitress refills their ice-waters.

"What did you have for breakfast, Morg?"

"I did not eat breakfast this morning."

"Me neither."

They high five. Fist bump. Pistol point at one another.

"My mother."

"Nurse Jackie."

"Made another prediction."

"Her last one. About flip-flops. Was dead on."

"She sees it. Every day. In the emergency room."

"I only wear mine at the pool now. And at the gym. In the steamroom."

"Good girl, Morg."

"What's her new prediction?"

"Boys wearing their pants half-way down their hips."

"I don't want to hear this prediction."

"No. It's not gruesome. She just said…"

"What?"

"She just said that these boys. With their pants hanging low. On their hips. Are all walking bowlegged. To keep their pants from falling down. Damaging their gaits."

"Shit. She's so right."

"These boys. They're all going to need their hips replaced. When they're forty."

They return their attention to the menus. Gabby has made it to the back cover. Morgan is still on the back inside cover.

"Morg."

"Yes."

"You've got a CSI name."

"What are you talking about?"

"Like. Get this dead body. To the morgue."

"Not funny."

Gabby waves to the waitress.

"Your favorite waitress is gaining weight."

"She better. If she wants to keep her job."

They place their orders. Separate appetizers. Soups. Salads. Entrees and desserts. All to be served at the same time.

Their waitress doesn't understand. "Everything at once?"

"Yes," says Gabby.

"Is that going to be a problem?" Morgan asks.

"Cook it all in the same pot" Gabby says.

Morgan says, "She joking."

When the food arrives—delivered by three servers—Gabby examines the soup. "It's greasy on top."

"Like at Morsel."

"I miss that place."

"The fattest waitresses. Ever."

"But this soup."

"I'm looking at your soup still. I haven't even looked at mine."

"This soup smells like cat."

"I smell cat, too."

"I wouldn't wash my balls in that soup."

"You sending yours back?"

"Of course."

"What about your salad?"

"I'm not looking at my salad until this soup is off the table."

Gabby tells the waitress that the soup is abysmal. She takes both soup bowls from the table.

"Can you bring the menus back, please," Gabby says.

The waitress says, "Certainly."

Morgan and Gabby watch the waitress walk away from their table and don't speak until she returns with two menus.

"I feel this would be so much easier. If that waitress weighed more."

"Maybe we can sneak a look at the kitchen help."

"That actually would make me hungry."

Gabby takes a picture of her salad with her phone.

"This salad does not look like the salad on the menu."

"The salad on the menu. Is a prom picture."

"I want to cry. All this food."

Gabby says, "Craig calls the clump of hair at the small of his back his other goatee."

"Is that the best you can do?"

"His new tattoo."

"On his neck?"

"It's infected."

"I should light up. See if they'd throw us out."

"Give the waitress that expired coupon."

"Do you still have the Nurse Jackie pictures? On your phone?"

"The flip-flop girl pictures."

Morgan says, "Yes."

Gabby brings up the photos on her phone. She passes the phone across the table to Morgan.

"I just lost my appetite."

"You're welcome."

Tonsure

This happened a very long time ago and it happened to me while I was sleeping and my father did it. It happened because I would, on occasion, hold my breath as I slept, at least, that's what I have always been told.

I had to be watched through the night and shaken awake from time to time and be reminded to take air. My parents took shifts, my small room lighted by a candle. They each kept an alert vigil, their eyes intent on their sleeping son. My mother would sometimes rest a light hand on my chest so she could know certainly that air was going into and leaving my lungs. I was keenly aware of their presence, even to the point of including them in my dreams as observers.

I was six years old. I knew all my prayers and what it meant when you crossed yourself. I was envious of my older brother, John, because he was an altar boy. My mother believed that he took his duties too lightly, and she warned him against letting his mind drift elsewhere when he served early Mass every Sunday morning.

While it's true that John would always grin when it came time for him to sound the bells at the moment of transubstantiation, when the bread and wine become the body and blood of Christ, it's necessary to understand that John, no matter

how hard he tried not to, grinned because the bells never failed to remind him of an approaching ice cream truck, not, as my mother feared, because his faith was less than serious.

But still, like my mother, I would chide John for his blasé approach to his responsibilities during the Mass, and I made a promise to myself and to my mother and father that when the time came for me to become an altar boy, I would surely understand the consequence of being an acolyte.

I was a very solemn little boy, too solemn, my father believed. I got ahold of advanced catechisms and set to memorizing each question and the proper response. I remember asking my father late one night, after he had pinched my cheek, shaken me slightly, and whispered for me to breath, if he would quiz me on what I had taught myself from a fifth grade catechism.

"Put that away," he said. "You're suffocating yourself with scripture."

My father liked his beer and he had a great many friends in the neighborhood pubs. It's safe to say that he had had a few that night, for no sooner had I closed my eyes did he leave my room and return with his straight razor and a lathered brush. While I slept he shaved the crown of my head.

I think now of John's grin of consecration at the sound of the bells, and the way my shaven pate itched a week after the fact. Now, on the eve of my Profession, when I and the eight other Novitiates in my class gather in the rectory to be instructed on tonsure, I laugh at the idea of a little boy who held his breath while he slept until the night his father shaved a spot on his head, and of how he grew up to become such a happy priest.

Scale

Forrester Young wanted smaller cigarettes.

The prop man—everybody on the set called him Props—was summoned and the problem was explained. But Props didn't understand. He turned to his assistant, who was also his daughter. He said to her, "Aren't cigarettes cigarettes?"

"These cigarettes are too big for the frame," the director said. "Forrester's face is getting overwhelmed."

The prop man's daughter said, "Filterless."

"No," said Forrester Young. "No!"

What Props did back at his workbench was nip a quarter inch from both ends and conceal the tiny logo with a light brown paint. Then he traced on another logo a little higher up.

He showed the new, smaller cigarette to his daughter. She held up crossed fingers, ever hopeful. They left their cramped-but-neat workspace and headed for the set.

The director studied the cigarette, comparing it to his brand. But he offered no comment as he passed it along to his assistant and sent for Forrester Young.

When Forrester Young emerged from his trailer, he was given the cigarette. He asked for a mirror. The makeup lady held up a small mirror, and Forrester Young brought the cigarette to his mouth and pretended to smoke. He took his mark and told the director he was ready for a take.

The closeup camera was put into position. The director asked for quiet on the set. Props lit the cigarette for Forrester Young with a disposable lighter. The director whispered, "Action."

"Listen to me, baby," Forrester Young said to the female lead who wasn't really there because she hadn't been cast yet, but who was going to be a blond and would be edited into the scene later on. "I have to go away for awhile. It isn't..."

But before he could say another word, laughter erupted on the set. There was brown paint on Forrester Young's lips.

Props turned his visor around catcher's style and brought the overhead light down closer to his left shoulder.

His daughter stood behind him, watching. He could hear her breathing. He was frequently asked to make miniature versions of common household items, like telephones, milk cartons, cameras. The reduced scale of a given prop—a doctor's stethoscope, a police officer's firearm, a judge's gavel—had a way of making a smallish actor appear full-size on screen.

Props pinched the tobacco out of a cigarette without tearing the paper and removed the filter. He stood the empty paper cylinder on its end beside the pile of tobacco and turned his attention to the filter.

With a sharp razor, he sliced into the filter. The way the tightly wound cotton fiber expanded and pushed through its wrapping reminded him of how his morning newspaper unfolded itself after he'd roll the elastic off of it.

Forrester Young had said the cigarette not only had to be smaller lengthwise, it also had to be smaller in diameter. As Props hollowed out the filter, he heard Forrester Young's deep resonating voice in his ear, carefully instructing him, telling him exactly how much filter to leave, how to repack the tobacco, close the opened filter and piece together the new cigarette. Once done, he set to taking apart and making a second smaller cigarette.

In his driveway, Props—his name was Martin Fahey—told his daughter he wanted to stay in the car for a few minutes longer. She had driven home that night because they took turns every other day and it had been her turn. Before she got out of their car she asked her father if he wanted her to sit with him.

"No," he said. "I'll be in in a minute. I just feel like we got home too soon today."

His daughter said, "I didn't go over the limit."

He smiled at her and told her she should go inside.

He found a book of matches in the glove compartment. He lit the second smaller cigarette that he had made, remembering how pleased Forrester Young had been with his cigarette and how well the scene came off and how, years ago, you used to be able to smoke in movie theaters. He once made it a point to see every movie that he worked. And, really, people smoked in movie theaters. He smoked a pipe back then, like his father, but he gave it up for Lent and found that he didn't miss it.

Analog

I was nine when this model came out. I remember wanting one. The *idea* of a stereo receiver with separate components—turntable, cassette tape, maybe even reel-to-reel tape player—was so much cooler than our awful one-piece hi-fi , with the tape-eating tape-player, the warped turntable, and the built-in tinny speakers. My mother said I was too young. Even if I had saved enough to buy the receiver, where would I get the money for the other components and the speakers, all sold separately. I called my father late one night—I didn't remember that it was even later at night where he was—and he told me that he would discuss it with my mother. "Which means no," I shouted into the phone. Walnut finish. Front facing is a pearlized appliqué that has circular patterns etched in it. The sides are vented in neatly cut slats. The man having the yard sale says, "She runs hot." I get her into the basement without my wife seeing. The packing on the bottom of her original box survived, styrofoam hard as wood and flaky. Her manual is in English only. Her console is presented in photographs with a woman's hand pointing to its features in each detail. She has two pin meters on the right. She's almost facial on the left, the alignment of three knobs: two level eyes and a nose between, slightly below a tiny open mouth in the form of her headphone

jack. She also has a set of toggles, for switching on additional speakers. And two lighted buttons. The word MONO is under the mono button (I still don't know why mono was an option after stereo was invented!). She has several input types on the rear panel, (5 volt, 12 volt, slurry, full-toothed, etc.) and one that looks like a scuzzy port. And what I was looking for: input for components (turntable, tape, and one that's labeled other) and the speaker hookups. The power cable is black, a replacement, I can tell. I have not plugged her in yet. I will clean her again tomorrow and read the manual again. Then I will plug her in.

Head Heart Hands Feet

.

I.

The head likes to breathe. But the head likes a hat. The eyes
want to see. The eyes like to look. But the eyes need glasses.
The nose doesn't work. Can't smell a thing. But the head likes
to breathe. The mouth is silent. The mouth eats. The mouth
drinks. The mouth drinks too much. The mouth burps. The
mouth spits. The mouth inhales, holds it. The mouth exhales.
The head remembers. The mouth speaks. The ears hear the
speaking. The eyes tear. The nose sniffles, recalling a sneeze. The
head can't breathe. The head wants its hat. The head breathes.
The mouth wants a mustache, a roof. The chin wants a beard,
to wear like a hat. The ears carry earrings. The eyebrows are
impressive but immobile. The eyes speak things unintended.
The eyes never shut up, not even in blinking. The throat red-
dens. The cheeks blush. The head wants to close the eyes. The
head wants to sleep. The head wants to dream. The head needs
a pillow.

In the town square, Haupt's ex-wife makes a statue of his
limitations, pants down around his ankles, dong out, a half-
aroused bird perch. A three-to-five moai head-to-body ratio,

his oversized face not so much chiseled as hacked. Broad nose and wide chin and square ears set low. His eyes bulge like those of a child actor, pure dope. "Yes, it's me," says Haupt. "Made with her own aggrieved hands, and lit from below so I can cast no shadow."

II.

The heart adores its candy counterpart. The heart counts the hours until St. Valentine's Day. The heart has a sweet tooth. The heart does its job in pursuit of a sugarcube. The heart falls in love through a magical process of giggles and desserts. The heart has wings of chocolate. The heart swims throughout the body in sweet syrup. The heart builds a wall of fudge. The heart remembers its first cookie. The heart calls everything traffic— muscle, bone, integument—all sweet traffic.

The woman who answers Coraggio's advertisement for a nude model says her name is Elise. Her face is pleasant enough and her figure is good. When Coraggio asks her if she had any trouble finding his studio, she says, "I am a prostitute. I know these streets." She requests her payment up front. She does not feel like bathing. She disrobes and stands herself in the light. She looks past Coraggio, at his paint brushes and then at a box of soft chocolates on his dresser. She smiles at Coraggio. Her teeth are a horror movie. He fetches the box for her and she helps herself to three sweets. Coraggio instructs her to face the other way. She has an acceptable number of moles on her back, the largest of which is in the shape of a heart.

III.

The hands speak. The hands conduct. The hands are machinists. The hands are musicians. Surgeons have hands. The

hands—what are you holding in your hands? The hands count on their fingers. The hands read their palms. The hands fold in prayer. The hands learn chopsticks. The hands search pockets. The hands remember pinching. The hands don't mind their fingernails being bitten because they relish the face-time. The hands take care of themselves. The hands take care of nearly forty percent of all greetings and over fifty percent of all farewells. The hands recite the mechanical alphabet.

Hender makes a fist with each hand and shadowboxes. A half dozen left jabs. A right cross. He works up a snort. He ducks. His hands are taped and his headgear is on. He bites into his mouthpiece. More combinations. His next fight is two weeks away. Got to train. Rocks in his hands. His hands are big. His hands are fast. At night when he sleeps he is always a boy in his dreams. Hender can't think about that boy now. That boy never set foot inside a gym before. Never hit a heavy-bag. Never let his back rest against the ropes to take a few punches. That boy has trains in his little hands—looking for another kid to play with. That boy never made a fist.

IV.

The feet ignore one another as best they can. The feet acknowledge their parallel partnership, but that is all. Each foot has its own enterprise of heel, arch, and toe. Each foot is incorporated from the ankle down. The feet are alive in stride and most happy in dance. The feet wish for more opportunities to kick. Feet concentrate hardest when skating. In order, male feet prefer: Boots, half-boots, oxfords, sneakers, loafers, moccasins, slippers, sandals, flip-flips. Female feet are like this: Flip-flops, sandals, flats. Female feet acknowledge and accept other types of footwear—boots, sneakers, and high-heels—but female feet do not like boots, sneakers, and high-heels.

Pye's feet are still growing. Size 26. A half size bigger each year. A width now of GG. His feet are cold. Later in the day, Pye will walk to the village to keep two appointments. The first appointment is with his podiatrist, Dr. Wick, who will dig and scrape away at the score of plantar warts on Pye's heels. The second appointment is with Musil the Cobbler for a new fitting. Before she died, Pye's mother knit him a supply of socks. She labeled the socks with his successive birthdays through his fortieth. Each set of socks accounted for the year's new growth. The thought of his mother makes Pye wobble when he stands. He misses how she tended after his feet each night and told him he would have to find a special wife to take on this job after she passed. Pye's village is on a hillside that is under snow nine months each year. Exiting his cottage, Pye stares down the long path to the village. The snow is panked but still soft in spots. Pye's snowshoes stand taller in the snow than those belonging to his brothers and father.

The Kennedys

Noah Kennedy, four years old, is drunk again. Due to an acid-base enzyme imbalance in the lining of his mouth, his saliva instantly ferments all liquids to alcohol.

Megan Kennedy is called megaphone because she doesn't need one.

Mrs. Kennedy recalls listening to Noah crying in his crib at night. He was almost two and he could say thirsty. He pronounced it fursty.

One day in early September, Mr. Kennedy will come home from work and tell Mrs. Kennedy that he'd seen his first school bus of the season, and that will signal to her that she should begin fixing him whiskey highballs after dinner instead of vodka tonics.

The year he starts eighth grade, Lucas Kennedy begins putting his father's whiskey in his soda after school. His first mixes are purposely weak. But before long he is mixing doubles and downing them. He raises his soda can in Noah's direction and says, Cheers, little dude.

Mrs. Kennedy told the obstetrician that Noah's breath smelled like beer. The doctor laughed. Later, Mrs. Kennedy overheard the doctor speaking about Noah with his the delivery nurse. He called Noah little baby bobble-head.

Noah's diagnosis takes several years. A doctor from North Carolina reading his case dubs the condition Bootlegger's Syndrome. This nifty coinage brings national attention to the doctor and then to Noah once his identity is deduced.

Megan's hand smells of puppetry, which has become for her a passion. She is sent back to the bathroom to wash her hands before dinner. Megan had been given puppets to see if she might find a new voice for herself.

If Noah acts silly, Mrs. Kennedy will give him a blood test. It is more accurate than the breathalyzer.

The signal in spring for vodka tonics is different every year— the sight of a particular migrating bird or some early perennials preparing to bloom, an item on the evening news about pitchers and catchers reporting to Florida for spring training.

The juiceboxes are in the locked cupboard. One six ounce juicebox is for Noah the equivalent of a fifth of bourbon for a full-grown man. Just a sip, Mrs. Kennedy tells Noah.

Megan brings her father's old turntable into her bedroom and begins playing *Tapestry* by Carole King. She plays side one over and over. Megan puts her puppets away for good. She mixes rubbing alcohol with fingernail polish remover and bubblegum flavored cough syrup. She drinks it from one of the souvenir shot glasses from Mr. Kennedy's collection.

At her first AA meeting, Mrs. Kennedy sits next to the only other woman her age. The woman's name was Joan and she immediately asks Mrs. Kennedy if she has any gum. She says, I feel just toothless without a stick of gum in my mouth.

Deep in the woods behind his house, Noah discovers naturally occurring train tracks running between two wide trees. He follows the tracks over the hill at the end of the woods and into a long clearing. He drinks water from a small mud puddle and looks up to see his brother Lucas in the clearing with a girl who is hiding her face. Lucas is holding two cans of soda. Noah walks backwards from the long clearing and counts his steps out of the woods to the backdoor of his house. He wants to be sure he will be able to find his way back to the puddle in the dark later that night.

William Walsh is the author of *Questionstruck, Unknown Arts, Pathologies, Ampersand, Mass.* (all from Keyhole Press), and *Without Wax: A Documentary Novel* (Casperian Books). His work has appeared in a number of journals, including *Annalemma, Artifice, LIT, Rosebud, Quarterly West, Caketrain, Juked, New York Tyrant*, and *McSweeney's Internet Tendency*. He is the editor of *RE:Telling* (Ampersand Books), a collection of literary fan fictions featuring the work of 30 authors.